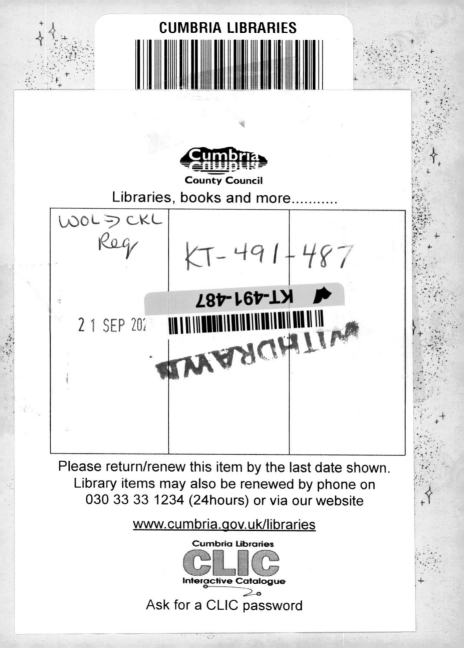

Sophie Kinsella

Mummy Fairy and Me

Fairy-in-Waiting

Illustrations by Marta Kissi

PUFFIN

PUFFIN BOOKS

UK | USA | Canada | Ireland | Australia
India | New Zealand | South Africa

Puffin Books is part of the Penguin Random House group of companies
whose addresses can be found at global.penguinrandomhouse.com.

www.penguin.co.uk   www.puffin.co.uk   www.ladybird.co.uk

First published 2018
001

Set in Bembo Infant MT Std
Text design by Mandy Norman

Printed and bound in Great Britain by Clays Ltd, Elcograf S.p.A.

A CIP catalogue record for this book is available from the British Library

ISBN: 978–0–141–37789–6

MIX
Paper from
responsible sources
FSC® C018179
FSC
www.fsc.org

Penguin Random House is committed to a
sustainable future for our business, our readers
and our planet. This book is made from Forest
Stewardship Council® certified paper.

For Phoebe and Saskia

CONTENTS

Meet Mummy Fairy and me

Hello. I'm called Ella Brook and I live in a town called Cherrywood with my mummy, my daddy and my baby brother, Ollie. I have blue eyes and dark brown hair. My best friends at school are Tom and Lenka. My worst enemy is Zoe. She lives next door and she's my Not-Best Friend. She is the meanest girl ever.

She looks mean even when she smiles.

So far, so normal.

But my family has a special secret, and I'm not allowed to tell anyone, not even my friends. My mummy looks normal, just like any other mummy . . . but she's not. Because she can turn into a fairy. All she has to do is stamp her feet three times, clap her hands, wiggle her bottom and say, 'Marshmallow' . . . and **POOF!** she's Mummy Fairy. Then if she says, 'Toffee apple,' she's just Mummy again.

My Aunty Jo and Granny are fairies too.

They can all fly and turn invisible and do real magic. Mummy and Aunty Jo also have a really cool wand called a Computawand V5. It has magic powers, a computer screen, an Extra-Fast Magic button, and Fairy Apps, Fairy Mail and Fairy Games!

The problem is that Mummy is still not that great at doing magic spells, even though she works really hard at her magic lessons on FairyTube with Fairy Fenella. But one day she's going to get everything right. And one day, when

I'm grown up, I'll be a fairy like her too. I'll have sparkly wings and my own Computawand.

Until then, Mummy says I just have to wait. So that's what I am. A Fairy-in-Waiting.

MONKERIDOO!
Mummy Fairy and the monkey business

One day I was watching Mummy Fairy learning magic from Fenella, her Fairy Tutor on FairyTube. She was learning a weather spell called Raineridoo, so I was watching from under an umbrella. Mummy Fairy was under a magic floating umbrella. I really wanted a magic floating umbrella too.

'You can use lots of different spells to stop the rain,' said Fenella, on the computer screen. 'Try "Normeridoo" with the code 4–5–2. It's a very useful spell.'

Mummy Fairy pressed 4–5–2 on her Computawand and said, **'Normeridoo!'** and at once the rain stopped.

When Mummy had finished the lesson and was back to normal, I sighed and Mummy looked at me.

'What's wrong, Ella?' she said.

'I'm tired of being a Fairy-in-Waiting,' I said. 'I want to be a *real* fairy and do *real* magic and save the day.'

Mummy laughed. 'Every little fairy girl thinks that,' she said. 'Never mind.

9

You'll get your chance. Now, what can we do to cheer you up?'

'Go roller-skating with Lenka and Tom?' I said. 'They're meeting at the park.'

'Oh dear,' said Mummy Fairy. 'I'm afraid we can't. We're going to lunch with Daddy's boss, Mr Lee. But that will be fun too!'

I didn't believe her. Then Daddy came in.

'Time to get ready for the lunch,' he said. 'Mr Lee is very important, so we must all look very smart.'

Now I *knew* the lunch wouldn't be fun.

10

I put on my best dress, and Mummy did my hair. She was trying to do French plaits. But Ollie kept pulling her arm, and she kept dropping bits of hair.

'Be *good*, Ollie!' I said, but I don't think Ollie knows what 'good' means.

'Right,' said Daddy, striding in. He was wearing his smartest shirt and a dark blue spotted tie. 'Are we all ready? Let's get in the car.'

Mummy reached for a ribbon, then dropped my plait again. 'Oh dear,' she said. 'I think I need some help.' She stamped her feet three times, clapped her hands, wiggled her bottom and said, 'Marshmallow' . . . and **POOF!** she was a fairy.

When Mummy turns into a fairy, she still looks like Mummy – but an even more beautiful Mummy. The sunlight was gleaming on her wings and her dress was all sparkly and her silver crown shimmered.

She waved her Computawand, pressed a code – *bleep–bleep–bloop* – and said, 'Plaitseridoo!'

A moment later, my hair was in the neatest, most beautiful plaits I'd ever seen, tied with red ribbons in bows.

'Mummy Fairy!' I said. 'These are brilliant! You're so clever! Look, Daddy!'

But when I looked at Daddy, I giggled.

Normally Daddy has short brown hair. But now he had long brown plaits with pink bows. I've never seen a daddy with plaits and pink bows before.

Mummy had long plaits too. Even Ollie had long plaits. We all had plaits.

'What!' said Daddy in horror when he saw his plaits in the mirror. '*What* have you done to me? I look like a little girl!'

'Oops,' said Mummy Fairy. 'I don't know how *that* happened. I'm sure I said the right spell.'

She quickly scrolled through the Spell App on her Computawand, then stopped and said, '*Here* we are.' She pressed in a code and said, **'Haireridoo!'**

At once we all had normal hair again.

But Daddy was still frowning. 'This lunch is important,' he said. 'I don't want

16

anything to go wrong. So I have a special rule for today. No magic.'

'No magic?' said Mummy Fairy.

'That's right.' Daddy sounded very firm. '*No magic*.'

★

All the way to Mr Lee's house, Mummy didn't do any magic. Even when the sat-nav broke and we got lost, Mummy didn't do a spell. She just asked a nice lady the way.

Mr Lee's house was very big, with an enormous garden and a little wood at

17

the end. Mrs Lee took me and Mummy
and Ollie round the garden and back again
while Daddy and Mr Lee were talking.

At the back of the house was a wooden
perch for a bird, but it was empty.

'Have you got a pet
bird?' I asked, and Mrs
Lee started blinking.
She had tears in her
eyes.

'Oh dear!' said Mummy. 'Are you all right, Mrs Lee? What's happened?'

'I have a parrot called Ben,' said Mrs Lee. 'I love him very much. But he's flown away! He's never done that before. I think he was getting bored.' She looked even sadder. 'Maybe I'll never see him again!'

Mrs Lee blew her nose and went into the kitchen to cook the lunch. I could smell something yummy cooking. I thought Mrs Lee was a very kind lady and I felt very sorry for her. If I had a parrot as a pet I wouldn't want it to fly away.

'Do you want to play, Ella?' asked Mummy.

'No,' I said. 'I want to find Mrs Lee's parrot for her.'

'I agree,' said Mummy. 'Let's go and look.'

We searched all the flowerbeds and trees. But we couldn't see a parrot anywhere. Then we looked at the wood at the edge of the garden.

'Maybe Ben went into the wood,' I said.

'We'll *never* find him in there.'

'It's no use,' said Mummy. 'We'll have to use magic.'

'But Daddy said no magic,' I said.

'I know.' Mummy thought for a moment. 'I think he meant, *No magic unless there's a lost parrot*. I'll be super careful. No one will know.'

'Mummy, can I do the magic?' I begged. 'Please?'

Mummy smiled kindly. 'I'm afraid not, Ella. But you can be my special helper. First of all, make sure no one can see us.'

I checked carefully everywhere, but we were alone. Then Mummy stamped her feet three times, clapped her hands, wiggled her bottom and said, 'Marshmallow' . . . and **POOF!** she was Mummy Fairy.

She pressed a code on

her Computawand – **_bleep-bleep-bloop_** – and said, **'Beneridoo! Finderidoo! Flyeridoo!'** Then she grabbed my hand.

The next minute we were flying through the air. I had never flown before and the air felt really cold and whooshy.

The ground seemed very far away and I held tightly on to Mummy. We flew into the wood and landed under a tree. Then we heard a sound. **_Squawk!_**

'The parrot is in the tree!' I said. 'We've found him! How shall we get him?'

'We mustn't startle him,' said Mummy Fairy, 'or he may fly away. I will fly up very slowly and try to catch him.'

She rose up into the air very

quietly and I watched her.
Then I heard that sound
again: **squawk!**

'Ben saw me,' Mummy
Fairy called down, 'and
he's flown to another branch.
He's a very cheeky parrot. Ella, your time
to help has come. Are you ready?'

'Yes!' I said. 'What shall I do?'

'I think you should climb the tree.
Between us, we can catch him.'

I looked up at the tree. It was very high,
with great big branches.

'Don't worry, Ella,' said Mummy Fairy, her eyes twinkling. 'I'll give you some magic help. You'll need super-strong legs.'

'OK!' I said, feeling excited. Maybe I couldn't do magic spells yet – but I could still catch Ben and save the day.

Mummy Fairy pressed a code on her Computawand – *bleep-bleep-bloop*. **'Climberidoo!'** she shouted.

I looked at my legs to see if they were changing yet. They *were* changing. They were getting very brown and hairy. I looked at my arms. They were brown

26

and hairy too. What was happening? Was
I still a little girl?

I looked at Mummy Fairy and
screamed. She had turned into a monkey.
Did that mean I was a monkey too? Ollie
was staring up at us with big blue eyes.

'Mummy Fairy!' I said in a monkey
voice. 'You've turned us both into
monkeys!'

'Oops,' said Mummy Fairy – and she
had a monkey voice too. 'I don't know
how *that* happened.' She put down the
Computawand, jumped up on to a branch

and swung by her tail. 'Hey, look what I
can do.'

'*I* want to have a go!' I said. '*Monkeridoo!*'
I jumped up too, and we both swung by

28

our tails. I scampered up to the top of the tree and looked right over the wood, but I couldn't see Ben the parrot. Then I leaped to another tree and swung by my tail again. Being a monkey was fun.

Then we heard a bell ring and I gasped.

'Mummy, it's lunchtime!' I said. 'Quick, change us back into people.'

'But where's the Computawand gone?' said Mummy Fairy. 'And where's Ollie?'

Then we saw him. He was heading off through the wood, holding the Computawand.

'Oh no!' cried Mummy Fairy. 'Chase him!'

We ran after Ollie on our monkey hands, and Mummy Fairy had nearly reached him . . . when all of a sudden Mrs Lee appeared through the trees. At once Mummy Fairy dived behind a bush and pulled me with her. I was breathing very fast. I didn't want Mrs Lee to see us.

'Hello, young man,' said Mrs Lee to Ollie. 'What are you doing all alone?'

She looked around for Mummy and me, but we kept very still behind the bush.

'Weezi-weezi-weezi!' said Ollie, and he pointed towards the bush, but Mrs Lee couldn't understand him. I was very glad that Ollie couldn't talk.

'That's a very smart phone,' said Mrs Lee, and she took the Computawand from him. Luckily it had turned itself off so now it looked like a normal phone. 'It must belong to your mummy. Let's go and have some lunch.' And she carried Ollie away towards the lunch table in the garden.

Mummy Fairy and I looked at each other. This was awful! What could we do?

We were monkeys, and Mrs Lee had the Computawand.

'We need to get the Computawand back,' said Mummy Fairy. 'Otherwise we'll be monkeys forever. Follow me, Ella. And when we see the others, pretend to be a real monkey. Do monkey things. Be naughty.'

'Be naughty?' I said. 'On purpose?'

'Yes,' said Mummy, and her monkey eyes twinkled. 'Just this once you can be as naughty as you like.'

We crept through the garden and up to

the lunch table. Mrs Lee was the first to
see us, and she gasped.

Mummy Fairy leaped on to the table.
'Ooh-ooh-ooh-ah-ah!'
she cried, and threw a bread roll at Mr
Lee. Then she put her monkey fingers up
Daddy's nose, and he sprang up from the
table. Mr and Mrs Lee screamed.

I jumped on to the table and screeched.
I ran up and down. Then I played with
Mrs Lee's hair and stuck my tongue out
at her. Mr Lee leaped up and tried to
catch me.

'**Help!**' said Mrs Lee. 'Did
they come from the zoo?'

'Did they come from the circus?'
said Mr Lee.

I was throwing salad around.
I *loved* being a naughty monkey.
Then I saw Daddy. He was looking
straight at me. Then he looked at
the Computawand on the table.

Then he looked at Mummy.

He knew it was us.

'Ooh–ooh–ooh–ah–ah,'

I said to him. I pointed to the
Computawand with my monkey
hands. What I meant was, *Give us the
Computawand quick, Daddy!*

Daddy understood. He picked up the
Computawand and waved it at Mummy
as if he was trying to shoo her away.

'Go away, monkey,' he said. 'Go away.'

Mummy Fairy grabbed the
Computawand and ran away.

Mrs Lee gasped. 'That monkey stole your phone!'

'Don't worry,' said Daddy. 'I'll chase it.'

Mummy Fairy and I ran off into the wood, and Daddy ran after us. He looked very cross.

'I thought I said no magic,' he said. 'That's what we agreed. All I wanted was to have a nice, simple lunch. And now look – you're monkeys.'

'I'm sorry,' said Mummy Fairy. 'We were trying to find Mrs Lee's lost parrot. I'll change us back. No problemo.'

She waved her Computawand, pressed
a code – **bleep-bleep-bloop** – and said,
'Unmonkeridoo!'

I could feel the spell working.
My hairy legs were changing
and I was getting taller.
A lot taller. And bigger.

'*What?*' shouted
Daddy.

I looked down and
gasped. I wasn't a monkey any
more – I was an elephant!
And so was Mummy Fairy.

38

I had a trunk! And great big feet! I picked an apple off a tree with my trunk and gave it to Daddy. Maybe being an elephant was quite fun.

But then I started to worry. What if Mummy couldn't change me back into a little girl? How could I be an elephant forever? I wouldn't be able to go to school. I would sit down on my chair and it would break. I decided I really, *really* didn't want to be an elephant.

'Mummy Fairy!' I said in a trumpety elephant voice. 'Do another spell!'

'Oops,' said Mummy Fairy, and her voice was trumpety too. 'Sorry about that. Let me try again.' She tried to use her trunk to press in another code, but the

Computawand fell to the ground. 'This is tricky,' she said. 'How do elephants do it?'

'They don't do magic,' said Daddy with a sigh. He handed the Computawand back to Mummy Fairy. This time she managed to press the code – **bleep-bleep-bloop**.

'**Unelephanteridoo!**' she trumpeted.

The magic was working again. I was getting shorter and shorter. I wasn't an elephant any more . . . but I wasn't a little girl either.

I was a penguin. And so was Mummy
Fairy.

'Penguins?' said Daddy, staring at me
and Mummy. '*Penguins?* This is ridiculous!'

'I don't know how *that* happened,' said Mummy Fairy in a penguin honk.

I tried to walk over to Mummy Fairy, but I could only waddle. I *really* didn't want to be a penguin. I would have to go and live in the snow and only eat fish.

'Hello?' I could hear Mrs Lee calling through the wood. 'Are you there? Are you all right?'

We all looked at each other. Being monkeys was bad enough. But being penguins was even worse.

'My spells aren't working!' said

Mummy Fairy to Daddy. 'I don't know *what* to do.'

Then I had an idea.

'Mummy Fairy –' I began.

But Daddy said, 'Not now, Ella!'

'But I know which spell you should use!' I said.

He and Mummy Fairy both turned and stared at me.

'Use the Normeridoo spell!' I said. 'Code 4–5–2. Remember?'

'Yes!' exclaimed Mummy Fairy. 'What a good idea!'

44

She waved her Computawand, tapped out the numbers 4–5–2 with the end of her flipper and said, '*Normeridoo!* Please! Please work!'

I could feel myself getting bigger. My hair came back.

My flippers became arms.

My beak became a nose. I was a little girl again.

'Thank goodness,' said Daddy. He grabbed me and Mummy Fairy and gave us a hug. 'Now, absolutely *no more magic.*'

'Ella, you are a brilliant Fairy-in-Waiting,' said Mummy Fairy. 'You saved the day for everyone.'

I felt all light and happy. I had saved the day!

'Thank goodness for Ella,' said Daddy, and he gave me an extra-big hug. 'Now, can we have lunch like a normal family? Just for once?'

'Of course!' said Mummy Fairy. 'Toffee

apple.' And she changed back to normal Mummy.

At that moment Mrs Lee appeared through the trees. She looked very confused to see us all together.

'Hello!' she said. 'There you all are! What's going on?'

'Um . . .' said Mummy.

'Well . . .' said Daddy.

'*Squawk!*' came a voice from above. And down from the tree flew Ben the parrot. He was red and blue, and he flew straight over to Mrs Lee and

sat on her shoulder.
'Ben!' cried Mrs
Lee. 'You found
my Ben! Thank
you so much!' She
stroked his head, and
he rubbed his beak against her. 'Now
come and have lunch,' she said to us. 'You
deserve it!'

We walked back to the table and sat
down with Ollie and Mr Lee.

'You'll never believe it,' said Mr Lee, 'but
we just had two monkeys in the garden!'

'No!' said Mummy, sounding very surprised. 'Real monkeys?'

'Yes!' said Mrs Lee. 'They were very naughty monkeys but they were funny too. I'm so sorry you missed them, Ella. Perhaps they'll be back. I've no idea where they could have come from . . .'

'Well, I hope they *don't* come back,' said Daddy, smiling at me. 'I can do without any more monkey business.'

Just then, Ben flew on to my shoulder. His claws were sharp, but I liked it. It felt funny, having a parrot on my shoulder.

49

I had thought this lunch would be boring, but it was so much fun. I couldn't wait to tell Tom and Lenka about the parrot. Maybe one day I could have a parrot as a pet. And we could play pirates or hide-and-seek together.

'I am going to buy Ben some parrot toys,' said Mrs Lee. 'Then he won't be bored.'

'**Squawk!**' said Ben, into my ear. He looked at me as though he was wondering why I wasn't a monkey any more.

After lunch I did some drawing in my book. I drew Ben in the tree, with his red and blue feathers. And as I drew I thought about being a monkey with furry legs. I thought about being an elephant with a long grey trunk, and a penguin with flippers. And I thought that what I *really* liked being, most of all, was a little girl.

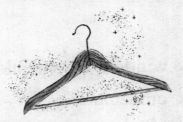

STOPERIDOO!
You can't stop
a magic wardrobe

One day we were out shopping when Mummy stopped dead and said, 'Wow! That's amazing!'

I looked around quickly, in case it was something *really* amazing, like a bath full of jelly beans, or a real live robot. But it was only an antiques shop with a big clock in the window. How could anyone call a clock 'amazing'?

Antiques are old furniture and things that smell dusty and don't work. You can't touch them or sit on them or play with them, even if it's a doll or a rocking horse. Mummy says that antiques are special, like treasure. She loves old cupboards and vases and pictures. Daddy doesn't. He calls antiques 'junk' and stands at the door of the shop, looking at his phone.

We all followed Mummy into the shop

and watched her looking at the clock.
Then she looked at some candlesticks
and plates. Everything looked boring to
me, especially the plates. Plates are only
interesting if they have yummy food on
them, like spaghetti bolognese.

Then Mummy cried out again, 'Wow!
That's amazing!'

By now, she was at the back of the
shop, looking at a big wooden wardrobe.
It had little legs, and a picture of a tree
painted on it.

Actually it *was* amazing. I had never

seen a wardrobe like it before. I looked at the picture and wondered who had painted it.

'It's beautiful,' said Mummy. 'We must give it a home.'

Daddy looked up from his phone. 'It's very big,' he said. 'And the door is falling off.'

'We'll mend it,' said Mummy.

Daddy looked at the wardrobe.

He didn't seem happy. 'Do we need another wardrobe?' he said.

'We'll keep our extra jumpers in it,' said Mummy. 'It's fabulous.'

When Mummy says things are fabulous, we always buy them.

★

When the wardrobe was delivered, it seemed even bigger than it looked in the shop. The men heaved it in through the door and up to the spare room, while Mummy followed them, saying, 'Isn't it beautiful?'

When the men had left, Mummy said,

'Now, we must mend this door.' She looked around. 'Where's Daddy gone?'

A text bleeped on her phone. Mummy read it and looked a bit cross.

'Daddy has suddenly decided to take Ollie to the supermarket,' she said. 'Well, never mind. I will mend the door myself.'

Mummy got out the toolbox. She put a scarf round her hair. She made herself a cup of tea. She took out the screwdriver and looked at it. Then she put it down. 'Magic is better,' she said. She stamped her feet three times, clapped

59

her hands, wiggled her bottom and said,
'Marshmallow' . . . and **POOF!** she
was a fairy.

I was excited to watch Mummy Fairy
fix the wardrobe, although I hoped
nothing would go wrong.

'Have you ever done any mending
spells before?' I asked her.

'Actually,' said Mummy Fairy, 'I am
very good at mending spells. I got a Gold
in my Mending and Building Spells Test.'
She pointed her Computawand at the
wardrobe, pressed a code – ***bleep–bleep–***

60

bloop – and said, 'Menderidoo!'

The wardrobe door came to life and set itself straight. The screwdriver floated into the air and fixed it with a screw. The door was perfect again.

'Well done, Mummy Fairy!' I said, and clapped my hands.

'There,' said Mummy Fairy. 'As good as new. What a beautiful wardrobe. Let's put all our jumpers in it.'

We fetched our thick winter jumpers, put them into the wardrobe and closed the door. But a moment later the doors

opened and the
jumpers flew out again
on to the carpet.

Mummy Fairy and I stared
at the jumpers.

'Did those jumpers just fly out
of the wardrobe by themselves?'
said Mummy Fairy.

We tried putting the
jumpers in the wardrobe
again, but again they flew
out. This time, one landed on
Mummy Fairy's head.

'Mummy Fairy!' I said. 'The wardrobe is magic!'

'Oh dear!' said Mummy Fairy. 'My spell must have been too strong. Let me fix it.' She got out her Computawand, but before she could use it we heard a voice coming from the wardrobe.

It was a very small, squeaky voice, and it said, **'Itchy.'**

'Itchy?' said Mummy Fairy.

'I think it means the jumpers,' I said. 'The jumpers are too itchy.'

I felt sorry for the wardrobe.

Itchy jumpers are horrible.

'This is ridiculous!' said Mummy Fairy. 'It is a wardrobe, not a person!' She pointed her wand at the wardrobe and said, '**Stoperidoo!** Now it will become normal again.'

But the wardrobe did not become normal again.

'**Itchy!**' it said. '**No jumpers!**'

Then it started walking towards the door on its little legs.

'Mummy Fairy!' I said. 'It's a walking, talking wardrobe!'

'Stop!' said Mummy Fairy. She pointed her wand at the wardrobe. **'Stoperidoo!'**

But the wardrobe didn't stop. It walked along the landing and started going down the stairs. **Thump, crash, thump!**

Mummy Fairy ran after it. She called, **'Stoperidoo! Stayeridoo! Stilleridoo!'** But nothing worked.

Mummy Fairy tried grabbing the wardrobe, but it was stronger than her.

It marched through the hall and out into the garden. Then it got into the paddling pool and started kicking its legs, making big splashes.

'Naughty wardrobe!' shouted Mummy Fairy. 'Come back! *Stoperidoo!*'

The wardrobe laughed a squeaky laugh — **'Hee-hee-hee!'** — and splashed even harder.

'None of my spells are working,' said Mummy Fairy. 'I think this wardrobe has its own kind of magic.' She walked up to the wardrobe and looked at it hard. 'Tell me the truth. Are you a normal wardrobe or a magic wardrobe?'

'Magic!' said the wardrobe in its tiny, squeaky voice. **'Magic wardrobe!'**

Suddenly it grew a pair of wooden

arms, with wooden hands. It waved at me
and I laughed.

'Look, Mummy Fairy!' I said. 'It's got arms!'

Mummy Fairy sighed. 'We can't have a magic wardrobe,' she said. 'We'll have to get rid of it.'

I couldn't believe it.

'But I love the wardrobe!' I said. 'It's fun!'

'Ella, we can't keep a magic wardrobe,' said Mummy Fairy. 'It will be too much trouble. I will lock it in the shed and then we will sell it.'

When Daddy came home, he and

Mummy had a talk. Then Daddy talked very sternly to the wardrobe and tied a rope round one of its legs. He made it walk to the shed, and locked the door. I was very sad. Before I went to bed, I ran to the shed. I looked through the window at the wardrobe.

'Goodnight,' I said. 'I wish you weren't so naughty. Then maybe Mummy and Daddy would let you stay.'

★

It was the middle of the night and I was dreaming about a fire engine. It was

71

going: 'Waaah, waaah, waaah.'

Then I woke up and realized it wasn't a dream. There was a real noise in the house. It sounded like: 'Waaah, waaah, waaaah.' I felt scared. What was the noise? I got out of bed and went to the door. I peeped out and saw Mummy and Daddy in their dressing gowns. They had been woken up too.

'What is that noise?' said Daddy.

'It's coming from the back door,' said Mummy.

We all hurried downstairs and Daddy

opened the back door. Outside, on the doorstep, was the wardrobe. It was crying very loudly: **'Waaah, waaah, waaah!'**

'It wants to come in,' I said. 'It's lonely. Poor wardrobe.'

'How did it get out?' said Daddy crossly.

'It has to go back in the shed,' said Mummy, and the wardrobe cried,

'Waaah!' even more

loudly.

Up and down our street, lights were

going on in houses. The wardrobe was waking everyone up.

'Please can the wardrobe come in?' I begged. 'It sounds so sad.'

'All right!' said Mummy to the wardrobe. 'You can come in for one night. But *that's all.*'

The wardrobe hurried into the house on its little legs. It went and stood next to the grandfather clock.

'Night night,' I said to the wardrobe. The wardrobe gave me a hug with its wooden arms, and I hugged it back.

'Now, be good,' said Mummy, and she wagged her finger at the wardrobe.

'**Good,**' said the wardrobe in its squeaky voice. '**Good, good, good.**'

Mummy, Daddy and I went back upstairs to bed.

'Well,' said Daddy. 'Let's hope we have a peaceful night.'

★

But we did *not* have a peaceful night. I was in the middle of a dream about flying with butterflies when I heard a loud noise:

crash!

I woke up straight away and jumped out of bed. I knew it was the wardrobe. I thought the wardrobe was being naughty downstairs. Maybe it was running about, or maybe it was playing with the furniture. Mummy and Daddy would be very cross and then they would never keep the wardrobe.

I decided to go downstairs and tell the wardrobe to be good.

I crept down the stairs. Then I stopped in surprise. The wardrobe was *not* being naughty. It was standing quietly next to

the grandfather clock.
There was another **crash!**
It came from the sitting
room. I was very scared.
What was making the
crashing noise?
I tiptoed over
to the sitting-
room door
and peeped
in. A man

in a mask was putting things into a sack. There was a broken vase on the floor, and a chair had been knocked over too. Those must have made the crashing sounds.

The man put Daddy's camera into his sack and then Mummy's silver clock. He was stealing our things! I felt very angry, but I didn't dare go in. Instead, I ran to the magic wardrobe.

'Wardrobe!' I said. 'There's a burglar! Catch him!'

The wardrobe hurried into the sitting room on its little legs. I heard a scuffly noise. Then the burglar came running out with the sack on his back.

'Wardrobe!' I cried. **'Help! Get the burglar!'**

The wardrobe came running very fast out of the sitting room. It chased after the burglar and grabbed him with its wooden hands.

'What?' shouted the burglar. He looked very surprised. He wriggled and hit the wardrobe, trying to get free. But the wardrobe was super strong. Then the wardrobe doors flew open. The wardrobe

stuffed the burglar inside itself. Its doors
slammed shut and the lock clicked.

The burglar was locked inside the wardrobe.

'Yay!' I cheered. 'Clever wardrobe!'

The next moment Mummy and Daddy appeared on the stairs. They both looked cross and sleepy. Mummy was yawning and Daddy's hair was sticking up.

'I've had enough!' said Daddy.

'What has that naughty wardrobe been doing *now*?' asked Mummy.

'It isn't naughty,' I told them. 'It's caught a burglar. It's a very, very *good* wardrobe.'

★

When the police arrived, Daddy opened
the wardrobe doors. The police looked
very surprised to see a burglar inside.
They pulled him out and put
handcuffs on him.

Click!

Then they took all our things out of his sack and gave them back to Mummy.

The burglar was very shocked. He told the police how the wardrobe had come to life and trapped him, but they didn't believe him. Then the police took the burglar away. Mummy made us some hot chocolate and we all sat in the hall and looked at the wardrobe.

'You can't send it away now,' I said. 'You can't. It's a good, clever, brave wardrobe. It's going to be a proper part of the family now.'

I patted the wardrobe, and it patted me back.

'I know it is,' said Mummy, and she gave a yawn. 'But it still needs training.'

'I'll train it!' I said. 'I'll look after it. Please? *Please?* It will be a really good wardrobe. I know it will.'

Mummy and Daddy smiled at each other.

'Do you think you can do it, Ella?' said Mummy. 'It's a big job, training a magic wardrobe.'

I thought about the wardrobe throwing

out the jumpers because they were itchy. I thought about it being lonely in the shed. I thought that if the wardrobe was really happy, maybe it would start being good all the time.

'Yes,' I said. I sipped my hot chocolate and smiled back at Mummy. 'I think I can.'

FLAKERIDOO!
Ice cream for everyone

We were going on holiday to France. There was going to be a beach and a swimming pool and boats to sail on. I had a new stripy swimsuit and a new hat, and even a new red suitcase with wheels. Wardrobe was left in charge of the house while we were away. Even though he doesn't like magic very much, Daddy said Wardrobe would be better than any guard dog.

Mummy Fairy was having a lesson from Fenella on FairyTube. They were doing magic packing.

She waved her Computawand, pressed a code – **bleep-bleep-bloop** – and said, **'Packeridoo!'** But all the clothes whirled around the room and landed on our heads.

'Oops,' said Mummy Fairy. 'Wrong code.' She pressed a different number and tried again: *'Packeridoo!'*

At once all the clothes folded themselves neatly and put themselves in our suitcases. Magic is very useful sometimes.

When Mummy's magic lesson was over, I said, 'I wish I could do the Packeridoo spell every day, instead of having to pack my school bag. I wish I could do magic *now.*'

'You'll be able to do it one day,' said

Mummy, smiling. She gave me a hug, then said, 'Have you packed your goggles?'

'Of course!' I said. 'I'm going to swim every single day.'

★

At the airport it was very, very crowded. There were people and trolleys and suitcases everywhere. We couldn't see

where to go. Daddy went off to ask someone, but he didn't come back for ages. Ollie dropped his teddy and started crying. A man ran over Mummy's foot with his trolley by mistake. More and more people were arriving and everyone was squashed. Mummy looked cross.

'There are too many people here!' she said. 'We'll never get to France!' She pulled us behind a trolley piled high with luggage so that no one could see. Then she stamped her feet three times, clapped her hands, wiggled her bottom and said, 'Marshmallow'. . . and **POOF!** she was Mummy Fairy.

She waved her Computawand at the crowds of people around us, pressed a code – *bleep–bleep–bloop* – and said, *'Empteridoo!'*

At once the airport was empty. There

92

were no people or suitcases or trolleys. There were no check-in desks or signs. There were no planes outside.

There was no airport at all! Just a big empty building and our family. Daddy came walking across the big empty space. He rolled his eyes.

'Don't tell me,' he said. 'Magic.'

'Oops,' said Mummy Fairy. 'I don't know how *that* happened.'

'There are no planes,' I said, and I started crying. 'Now we can't go on holiday!' I wouldn't be able to use my new suitcase or go swimming in my goggles.

'We *will* go on holiday!' said Mummy Fairy, and she gave me a hug. 'Don't worry, Ella. I will magic the airport back.'

'And then, maybe, put the Computawand away?' said Daddy. 'Just for a week.'

★

When we got to our hotel, I was very excited. There was a beach and a swimming pool and a big climbing frame. There was a sandpit for Ollie, and lots of sunbeds to lie on.

94

The best sunbeds were the blue ones by the sandpit. They had umbrellas with white fringes, and special tables and big comfy cushions. But another family had got them. They were French and they all had dark hair. There was a mummy and a daddy and a girl and a baby boy – just like our family.

They all wore sunglasses, even the baby. I thought they looked very cool.

'Tomorrow we will put our towels out early,' said Mummy. 'We will get those sunbeds.'

We swam and played all morning, and I wrote a postcard to Tom and Lenka. Then, after lunch, I went to the sandpit. Ollie was playing with the French baby, whose sister was there too. She had a really nice swimming costume with flowers on it.

'Hello,' I said. 'I'm Ella.'

''Allo,' said the girl. 'I am Cécile.'

Cécile was older
than me. She was twelve.
We played together all
afternoon and had loads
of fun. Cécile could do back
dives and hand stands.
We played diving for
coins together, and
sometimes she let
me win, and then
we had ice
cream.

'*Délicieuse!*' said Cécile, licking her ice cream. 'It means . . . delicious!'

Cécile's English sounded funny. Later, Mummy told me it was a French accent.

★

The next morning I saw Mummy on our balcony. She was holding our swimming towels and she had turned into a fairy.

'Mummy Fairy, what are you doing?' I asked. 'Daddy said no magic!'

'Shhh,' she said. 'Let's not wake Daddy.' She pressed a code on her Computawand

– *bleep–bleep–bloop* – and pointed at the towels. 'Sunbedseridoo!'

At once the towels flew off through the air. They looked like big birds with white flappy wings. I saw them land on the blue sunbeds by the sandpit.

'There,' said Mummy Fairy. 'Now we will have the best sunbeds.'

'What if someone moves our towels?' I said.

'They can't,' said Mummy Fairy, giving me a wink. 'Those towels have special magic now. No one can move them.

Toffee apple!' And she was normal again.

But when we got down to the pool, our towels had moved. They were on not-so-good sunbeds. Cécile and her baby brother, Pierre, and their mummy had the best sunbeds.

Mummy went up to Cécile's mummy and said, 'Excuse me. Our towels were on those sunbeds.'

Cécile's mummy smiled. She said, 'Our towels are there now.'

I knew Mummy was cross, but she didn't want to show it. She came back

to me and sat down on the not-so-good
sunbed. She looked at Cécile's mummy.

I went and played with Ollie and
Pierre in the sandpit. I helped them make
a great big sandcastle, and then they both
sat on it – **squash**. All the time, I
could see Mummy thinking hard.

The next morning, before breakfast, I
went on to the balcony again and saw
Mummy. She was watching the blue
sunbeds.

'Shhh,' she said. 'I'm waiting.'

Then an amazing thing happened.

Cécile's mummy came out on to the balcony below holding a pile of towels. She had shimmering wings, an emerald-green crown and a Computawand. She was a fairy, just like Mummy!

Cécile's mummy pressed a code on her Computawand – *blum-blum-blam* – and said a word I didn't understand.

At once her towels
flew through the
air and landed on
the best sunbeds.

'I *knew it!*' said Mummy.
Very quickly, she stamped her feet three
times, clapped her hands, wiggled her
bottom and said, 'Marshmallow' . . . and
POOF! she was a fairy.

She waved her Computawand at the
towels. '**Towelseridoo!**'

The towels started flying back through
the air. Cécile's mummy couldn't believe
her eyes. Then she looked up, saw Mummy
Fairy and gasped, '*Zut alors!*'

Mummy Fairy shouted,
'**Towelseridoo!**' again, and this time

our towels started flying towards the best sunbeds.

Cécile's mummy yelled something else, and her towels flew off too. They reached our towels, and all the towels started fighting in the air. They were wrestling, with the corners punching and poking each other.

I couldn't stop laughing because they looked so funny. Then suddenly I saw an old man on the ground below us. He was staring up at the fighting towels as though he couldn't believe his eyes.

'Careful!' I said. 'That man is watching!'

'Oops,' said Mummy Fairy.

'*Sacré bleu!*' said Cécile's mummy.

They both called their towels back to the balconies. The two mummy fairies stared at each other. Then they started laughing.

'Let us share the sunbeds,' said Cécile's mummy. 'And let us be friends. My name is Marie.'

★

That afternoon Mummy and Marie lay on their sunbeds next to each other. They talked and talked. Daddy and Cécile's

daddy talked too. Mummy and Marie
showed each other their Computawands
and told stories about when they were
at Fairy School. The two daddies talked
about when magic spells go wrong.
Cécile's daddy said that Marie had once
made the Eiffel Tower disappear by
mistake. My daddy laughed and laughed.

Ollie and Pierre were playing together
in the sandpit. I wanted to talk to Cécile,
but she was reading a magazine and I felt
a bit shy.

I said, 'I like your swimming costume.'

Cécile said, 'I made it with a magic spell.' She looked around to check that no one could see. Then she reached into her bag and pulled out a Computawand. 'This is mine,' she said. 'Do you have one?'

I couldn't believe it! Mummy always says I can't have my own Computawand until I am grown up and have been to Fairy School.

'No,' I said. 'I haven't got one.'

'You're not grown up enough yet,' said Cécile with a smug smile. 'Not like me. I can do lots of spells.'

I felt jealous. I wanted a Computawand like Cécile.

Then Mummy came over and I said, 'Mummy, look! Cécile has got a Computawand!'

Mummy looked astonished. 'Goodness!' she said. 'In our country, no children are allowed Computawands. It is against the Fairy Rule Book.'

'But we're not in our country now,' I said. 'Can I have a go?'

'No!' said Mummy. She didn't look very happy. 'Let's go down to the beach now.'

We went down to the beach and played in the waves, and Daddy pretended he was a shark. Ollie laughed and gurgled.

But all I could think about was the Computawand. I really, *really* wanted to have a go.

★

After lunch Mummy and Daddy went in the pool with Ollie. Cécile and Pierre were in the pool too, and so were their mummy and daddy. I was sitting on my sunbed, all alone.

Cécile's bag was on the ground and I could see her Computawand. I knew I shouldn't touch it. It wasn't mine. I wasn't allowed.

But I thought, *What if I just have one tiny go? Maybe no one will even notice.*

I picked up the Computawand. It was smaller than Mummy's, but the buttons looked the same. When I touched it, it started to glow and grew into a wand. I can bring a Computawand alive because I am a Fairy-in-Waiting, but I'm not allowed to do magic. Whenever I play with Mummy's Computawand, she turns off the magic function completely.

I tried to remember the codes that Mummy Fairy had learned from her magic lessons with Fenella on FairyTube. I remembered the spell for a vanilla Flake ice cream.

I thought, *A vanilla Flake ice cream would be yummy. I could eat it very quickly and no one would know.*

I pressed 4-3-2 – ***bleep–bleep–***

bloop. Then I waved the wand and said,
'Flakeridoo!'

But nothing happened. Had I done the
spell wrong?

Then I heard loud screams. I looked
round and gasped. The pool wasn't
blue any more – it was yellow. The
whole swimming pool was filled
with vanilla ice cream, with
chocolate Flakes sticking up
everywhere.

'**Yay!**' shouted a boy. 'An ice-cream pool! This is my best holiday *ever*!'

'This pool is freezing and icy!' shouted an old man angrily. 'I want my money back!'

No one could swim properly in the ice cream. Some children started licking it instead. Others dived into the ice cream with their mouths open. Mummy was holding Ollie and he started splatting ice cream into her face.

Everyone was going **slurp-slurp** in the ice cream. One girl was trying to eat six chocolate Flakes at once.

But then everyone began to get cold because ice cream is freezing. Pierre and Ollie started crying.

Suddenly Mummy looked up at me. I still had the Computawand in my hand. I tried to hide it quickly, but Mummy had seen it.

'Ella!' she shouted. 'What have you done?'

All the people in the pool were ice-creamy and cold. I had spoiled the holiday and I wasn't supposed to do magic and now Mummy would be very cross with me. I put Cécile's Computawand back in her bag as quickly as I could. Then I ran down to the beach and hid behind a deckchair. I wanted to hide forever.

★

When I heard Mummy calling me, I squeezed into a little ball. I didn't want her to find me. But she did. She sat down beside me and took my hand.

'Oh, Ella,' she said.

I started to cry, but I didn't look up.

'I spoiled the holiday,' I said.

'No you didn't,' said Mummy. 'Don't worry. I always bring Fairy Dust on holiday, and so does Cécile's mummy. We'll put everything right.'

'I'm sorry,' I said in a tiny voice. 'I wanted to be grown up and do proper spells.'

'You *will* be grown up and do proper spells,' said Mummy gently. 'But not yet. You're too young for a Computawand. I never want you to touch one again, not even mine, unless I've said that you can. Do you promise?'

'I promise,' I said.

'Cécile was showing off,' Mummy said. 'That wasn't her Computawand – it's an old one. Cécile is allowed to carry it,

120

but she is *not* allowed to do spells. Her mummy is cross with her for fibbing.'

'Oh,' I said.

'Now, tell me something,' said Mummy. 'What spell did you *want* to do?'

'I wanted a vanilla Flake ice cream,' I said.

'Good!' said Mummy. 'Look up, Ella.'

I looked up. Mummy was holding out a vanilla Flake ice cream to me.

'Here you are,' she said, and she gave it to me. 'You don't need to be a fairy to have an ice cream on holiday.'

Mummy hugged me and I hugged her back.

'Marie and I have decided to put away all our Computawands,' she said. 'For the rest of the holiday we will just be two normal families. Do you think that's a good idea?'

I thought about Mummy and the empty airport. I thought about the fighting towels. I thought about the ice-cream swimming pool and all the freezing people. And I smiled at Mummy.

'Yes,' I said. 'I think it's a very good idea.'

FLYERIDOO!
The best birthday party ever

One morning I woke up to see
Mummy and Ollie standing
by my bed with a bunch of balloons.
For a moment I didn't know what was
happening . . . then I remembered!
It was my birthday!

'Happy birthday, darling!' exclaimed

Mummy, and she kissed me. 'You have a very exciting day ahead of you. Waffles for breakfast, presents to open . . . and then this afternoon it's your party!'

'Weezi-weezi-weezi!' said Ollie, and he gave me a big gummy smile. I decided he meant, 'Happy birthday, Ella.'

★

The party was in a big hall. Mummy had invited everyone and made a pink cake and there was a magician. Mummy explained to me that the magician couldn't do *real* magic, only pretend magic. But it would still be good fun.

It was a fancy-dress party, and everyone wore a costume. I came as a clown and Lenka came as an astronaut. Tom came as a caterpillar.

'I wish I really *was* an astronaut,' said Lenka. 'I would fly to the moon.'

'I would be a space caterpillar,' said Tom. 'I would chase you around the moon.'

'And I would be a space clown,' I said.

We all chased each other around the room making space-monster noises. Then my Not-Best Friend Zoe arrived. She was dressed as a princess and she didn't join in the game. She just stood by the door and gave us a horrible look. Zoe is my Not-Best Friend because she says mean things and pushes

people. She waits until the teacher isn't looking, then she pushes you and runs away. Mummy says Zoe needs to grow up. I think Zoe just needs to stop pushing and being mean.

Mummy and Daddy were at the party too, dressed up like pirates. Aunty Jo was dressed as a cat, with ears and a tail. Granny was dressed as Granny.

The magician started and we sat down to watch, but he wasn't a very good magician. He made a coin disappear, but then he couldn't find it again. Then he did a trick with cards, but he dropped all the cards on the floor, slipped over on them and banged his head.

'Tragic,' said Aunty Jo, shaking her head.

'Can't he do any better than that?' said Granny.

'Shhh!' said Mummy. 'You'll hurt his feelings.'

The magician had a magic wand, but it didn't seem to work. He said, 'Abracadabra!' but nothing happened.

The magician looked very miserable. He tried to pull a rabbit out of a hat, but the hat was empty.

'I give up,' he said, and sat down on the floor. 'I can't find that rabbit anywhere.'

All my friends were laughing at the magician. Even Tom was laughing. I started laughing too. The magician wasn't very good at magic, but he was funny.

'Do some magic!' Tom shouted at the magician.

'I'm trying to!' said the magician. 'Magic is very hard!' He waved his wand, but nothing happened. 'See?' he said.

'Super tragic,' said Aunty Jo, and she raised her eyebrows at Mummy. 'Normal humans shouldn't try to do magic.'

'He looked good on the website,' said Mummy, looking worried.

'The children won't mind,' said Daddy. He looked at his watch. 'Is it time for tea yet?'

But Daddy was wrong about people not minding because then my Not-Best Friend Zoe came over. She was smiling, but in a nasty way.

'This party is rubbish,' she said. She said it quietly, in my ear. 'It's really, really rubbish.'

'It's not,' I said.

'Yes it is,' said Zoe. 'My party was much better. At my party, we had go-karts and hot dogs. Your party is *rubbish*.'

'Excuse me?' A loud voice interrupted her. 'This party is *not* rubbish!' It was Mummy, and she looked very fierce.

Zoe backed away. She looked a bit scared.

'This party is *not* rubbish!' agreed Aunty Jo. She looked fierce too.

'No, it's certainly *not*!' cried Granny. She looked at Mummy and Aunty Jo. 'Shall we?'

There was a pile of chairs at the side of

the hall. Granny, Aunty Jo and Mummy all went behind the chairs, where no one could see them. They stamped their feet three times, clapped their hands and wiggled their bottoms. I held my breath and watched them. 'Marshmallow!' said Mummy. 'Sherbet lemon!' said Aunty Jo. 'Extra-strong mint!' said Granny.

And . . . **POOF!** Suddenly all three were fairies with shimmering wings. Mummy Fairy was wearing her silver crown, Aunty Jo Fairy was wearing her diamond crown, and Granny Fairy was

wearing her golden crown with blue stones. When you become a grown-up fairy, you choose your Fairy Crown and you have it forever. Mine is going to be pink and silver with diamonds all over.

Daddy stared at them. 'Really?' he said. 'Is this a good idea? Everyone will see you!'

'They'll think we're in fancy dress,' said Aunty Jo.

'Just this once because it's Ella's birthday.' Granny Fairy winked at me. Then she pointed at the magician with her star wand.

'Spelleridoo!' she shouted.

At once blue sparks came out of the magician's ears, then red puffs of smoke.

'Ooh!' said everyone.

The magician waved his magic wand, and it played music. He waved it again, and it made bubbles.

He waved it again, and sweets came shooting out of the end.

'I'm magic!' he said.

'I'm really magic!'

The magician looked very excited.
He started waving his wand everywhere.
His toy rabbit turned into a real rabbit
and started hopping around the floor. His
cards built themselves into a tower, all by
themselves. A string of hankies came out
of his sleeve and started flying around the
room like birds.

'This is amazing!' said Lenka.

'It's brilliant!' said Tom, and he started
clapping.

Zoe didn't say anything, but she was watching with big, round eyes.

Then Aunty Jo waved her Computawand and shouted, **'Flyeridoo!'**

I could feel myself going up into the air. I felt like a bubble. I was flying! All my friends were flying too, and I heard them gasping and shrieking with excitement.

It felt like swimming in the air. We were
all laughing and kicking and waving at
each other.

Daddy and Mummy Fairy were flying
around holding hands. Daddy said, 'This
takes me back,' and he kissed Mummy
Fairy. He looked very happy. Sometimes I
think Daddy only *pretends* not to like magic.

'Yahoo!'
shouted Tom
as he floated past.
'This is the best
party ever!' He started
kicking a helium balloon.
'Let's play flying football!'
Everyone was flying
and kicking the helium
balloons. Ollie was flying
upside down, saying, **'Weezi-weezi-**
weezi!' The only person not flying
was the magician. He was sitting on the

floor, staring at his wand, saying, 'Am I dreaming? Am I really, truly magic?'

Then I floated over towards Mummy Fairy, Granny Fairy and Aunty Jo Fairy. They were standing by the tea table, looking at my pink birthday cake. Mummy Fairy seemed a bit cross.

'What's wrong with it?' she said to Granny Fairy and Aunty Jo Fairy. 'I made it myself.'

'It could be bigger,' said Granny Fairy.

'And yummier,' said Aunty Jo Fairy.

'And grander.'

'With more squidgy icing and silver balls and jelly babies,' said Aunty Jo Fairy. 'Shall I do it? I have a very good Cake Spell. It won a prize at the Fairy Fair.'

'No!' said Mummy Fairy, looking even crosser. '*I'll* do it!'

She pressed a code on her Computawand – **bleep–bleep–bloop** – waved it in the air and shouted, '*Cakeridoo!*'

At once the cake started to grow. It grew bigger and bigger and bigger.

'Stoperidoo!' said Mummy Fairy when the cake was as tall as me. But the cake didn't stop growing. 'Stop!' shouted Mummy Fairy. 'Stoperidoo!'

But the cake still didn't stop. It grew so big it nearly reached the ceiling. It was like a mountain of cake, covered in pink strawberry icing and silver balls and jelly babies. With everybody flying in the air, people started crashing into it, and pink icing splattered everywhere.

I suddenly remembered one of
Mummy's magic lessons with Fenella on
FairyTube. I flew up to Mummy's ear and
whispered, 'Mummy Fairy, try saying,
"Stoperidoo, cakeridoo." '

'Stoperidoo, cakeridoo!'
shouted Mummy Fairy, and at last the
cake stopped.

'Well done, Mummy Fairy!' I said
quickly.

'You did it!'

I wanted Granny and Aunty Jo to think Mummy Fairy was really brilliant at magic, because she is. At least, some of the time.

'Now it's *too* big,' said
Aunty Jo.

'It's just right,' I said.
'I wanted a cake this big.
Didn't I, Mummy Fairy?'

'But everyone's got
stuck in the icing!' said
Granny Fairy.

It was true. Everyone
who had crashed into the
cake was stuck. Now it was
a pink cake decorated
with children!

'Yum, yum, yummy!'

shouted Tom. His whole face was covered
in pink icing and he was licking it off.
'I love this birthday cake!'

Everyone was laughing and eating
the icing and throwing icing snowballs at
each other.

'It's the best cake ever,' I said, and I gave
Mummy Fairy a hug.

'Did I make the cake grow too?' said
the magician. He looked shocked. 'Am I
really that magic?'

We all stood around the mountain cake, and Mummy Fairy lit my candles, and everyone sang 'Happy Birthday'. The cake was too big to cut, so everyone just pulled bits off with their hands.

Then we all sat down and the magician read us a story, while Mummy Fairy, Granny Fairy and Aunty Jo Fairy cleared up the cake. Then Mummy Fairy said, 'Toffee apple!' Granny Fairy said, 'Flapjack!' and Aunty Jo Fairy said, 'Blueberry pie!' and they were all normal again.

As the magician finished the story,
Aunty Jo sprinkled a bit of Fairy Dust on
him so that he would forget all about the
magic he had seen. For ten seconds the
magician was very still. He had sort of
gone to sleep. Then . . .

'*Go!*' said Aunty Jo, and he woke up.

'What happened?' he said, blinking. 'Is
the party over? Did I do some magic? Did
it work?'

'I don't think you should try to do
magic any more,' said Aunty Jo. 'It's not
the job for you. Is there anything else

you've always wanted to do?'

The magician sighed. 'I always wanted
to be a train driver,' he said. 'Maybe I'll do
that instead.' He took his rabbit out of his
bag and looked at me. 'I won't need this
rabbit any more. Would you like it as a
birthday present?'

'Oh, yes! Yes please!' I said. I crossed my fingers and toes, and hoped Mummy would say yes.

'All right, Ella,' she said, smiling. 'You can keep the bunny rabbit.'

I was so, *so* happy. At last I had a pet of my own. I had a pet rabbit!

And then it was time for everyone to go home.

'This was the best party ever!' said Tom as he was putting on his coat. 'Ever, ever, *ever*.'

'No it wasn't,' said Zoe. 'My go-karting party was the best.'

'It wasn't,' said Tom, into my ear. 'Yours was, Ella.'

Zoe stared at me with small, cross eyes. She looked at me, then at Mummy, Aunty Jo and Granny.

'How did you make everyone fly?' she said. 'How did your cake grow so big? Are you *magic* or something?'

I didn't know what to say. I'm not allowed to tell anyone that Mummy is a fairy.

But luckily Granny heard Zoe. She came straight over and said, 'It was the magician. He has lots of special tricks up his sleeve. Now, go and get your party bag.'

'But your mummy had wings,' said Zoe. 'So did your aunt and your granny. They looked like fairies. Are they real fairies?'

'They were costumes!' said Aunty Jo. 'We're not really fairies, just like you're not really a princess.'

Then Zoe's mum came in through the door and Zoe rushed over to her.

'Ella's mummy was a fairy,' said Zoe. 'She was, she really was. She turned into a fairy. With wings.'

'Wonderful, darling!' said Zoe's mum. 'I do love fancy-dress costumes.'

'And we flew! And the birthday cake grew and grew. It was enormous. They did magic. Real, proper magic.'

'Marvellous!' said Zoe's mum. 'The magician must have had some very clever tricks. What a fun party. Have you said, "Thank you for having me"?'

Zoe got her party bag from Mummy
and said, 'Thank you very much for the
lovely party.' Then she came over and
looked at me again with her tiny, angry
eyes. 'I'm going to find out,' she said, in
a quiet voice that no one else could
hear. 'I know your mum's a real fairy.
And this birthday party was real magic.
Wasn't it?'

I thought about the magician, and the
blue sparks, and the bubbles, and the real
rabbit. I thought about flying through
the air, and the mountain cake. I thought

about everyone saying it was the best ever birthday party. And I smiled.

'Thank you for coming, Zoe,' I said. 'I hope you had a lovely time.'

TEST YOUR

Fairy Skills

Turn the page for lots of fun activities!

You can find all these activities at
www.puffin.co.uk/mummyfairy,
where you can print them out and test
your fairy skills again and again!

UNSCRAMBLERIDOO!

Uh oh! Ella borrowed Mummy's
Computawand and scrambled up these words!
Help solve the magical mayhem
by unscrambling them.

(Answers on page 167.)

★¹ NFYCA SEDSR

_ _ _ _ _   _ _ _ _ _

★² IFYRA TUDS

_ _ _ _ _   _ _ _ _

★³ FOTFEE PAPEL

_ _ _ _ _ _   _ _ _ _ _

FINDERIDOO!

Help Ella and Mummy Fairy find Mrs Lee's parrot!

(Answer on page 167.)

FILLERIDOO!

Can you work out what these words
from Ella's adventures are?

ACROSS

 Ella goes on one to France.

He performs at Ella's party, but
needs a little help.

 Mummy Fairy accidentally
turns Ella into one!

 Mummy Fairy brings one to life!

DOWN

Mrs Lee has one, but he flies away!

 Mummy's own Mummy Fairy!

 Ella and Cécile's mummies had a towel
fight over one of these!

(Answers on page 167.)

ICE CREAM RECIPE

You don't need a Computawand to
make ice cream – make your own at home
with this simple recipe! Just make sure you get a
grown-up to help, especially with using the whisk.
(They don't have to be a fairy!)

INGREDIENTS
- ★ One 397g tin sweetened condensed milk
- ★ 2 teaspoons pure vanilla extract
- ★ 600ml double cream, cold

FOR MORE FLAVOURS!
- ★ Chocolate: 150ml unsweetened cocoa powder
- ★ Strawberry: 300g strawberries, pureed
  (and sieved, if preferred)

METHOD

1 Place the condensed milk, cream and vanilla extract in a large bowl. Add your cocoa powder or strawberries here too if you want to make different flavours!

2 Whisk the mixture for around 5–6 minutes, until soft peaks form.

3 Spread the mixture into a freezer-proof dish or tub. Cover and freeze for about 8 hours, until firm. Transfer to the fridge for 15–30 minutes before serving to soften.

DESIGN YOUR FAIRY CROWN?

When Ella grows up she will be able to choose her fairy crown. Draw your own crown below – remember to colour it in!

ANSWERS

UNSCRAMBLERIDOO!

★1 FANCY DRESS ★2 FAIRY DUST ★3 TOFFEE APPLE

FINDERIDOO!

FILLERIDOO!

ABOUT SOPHIE KINSELLA

Sophie Kinsella is a bestselling author and the adventures of Ella and Mummy Fairy are her first stories for children. Her books for grown-ups have sold over thirty-eight million copies worldwide and have been translated into more than forty languages. They include the Shopaholic series and other titles such as *Can You Keep a Secret?*, *The Undomestic Goddess*, *My Not So Perfect Life*, *Surprise Me*, and *Finding Audrey* for young adults.

You can find out more about Sophie's books on her website:

www.sophiekinsella.co.uk